Mr Twiddle in
Trouble Again

Enid Blyton's Happy Days Series

Enid Blyton

Mr Twiddle in Trouble Again

Text illustrations by Stephen Dell
Cover illustration by Lesley Smith

AWARD PUBLICATIONS LIMITED

For further information on Enid Blyton please contact www.blyton.com

ISBN 1-84135-299-3

First published in *Don't Be Silly, Mr Twiddle* and
Well, Really Mr Twiddle 1949 & 1953 by George Newnes
This edition first published 1999 by Bloomsbury Publishing Plc

First published 2004 by Award Publications Limited

Published by Award Publications Limited,
The Old Riding School, The Welbeck Estate,
Worksop, Nottinghamshire. S80 3LR

Printed in India

Contents

Chapter 1

Mr Twiddle in Trouble Again

Mr Twiddle was sitting by the fire reading his paper. The windows were shut. It was nice and warm and cosy.

Then the cat pushed at the door, opened it wide, and strolled into the room. A cold draught at once blew down Mr Twiddle's neck.

He looked around, and then spoke crossly to Mrs Twiddle, who was sitting on the opposite side of the fireplace.

'Dear, I wish you'd teach your cat to shut the door after her. She comes in and leaves it wide open – and I have to get up and shut it.'

'You can't teach cats things like that,' said Mrs Twiddle, sleepily.

'You can teach dogs all kinds of tricks,'

grumbled Mr Twiddle. 'Shut the door, Puss!'

The cat sat down and washed itself. It always did that when it saw that Twiddle was cross. It knew it annoyed him.

'Oh, do get up and shut the door, Twiddle,' said his wife. 'There's such a draught.'

Twiddle got up, grumbling. He shut the door and came back to his chair. The cat was now lying on it, fast asleep.

'Look at that!' said Twiddle. 'It not only leaves the door open for me to shut, but takes my chair, too, and then pretends to be asleep.'

He turned the cat off his chair. It at once went to a window, and mewed. 'Let it out, Twiddle, dear,' said Mrs Twiddle.

'But it's only just come in,' said Twiddle, exasperated.

'Well, it wants to go out again,' said Mrs Twiddle.

So Twiddle got up, opened the window and let the cat out. He banged the window shut so hard that the cat leapt into the air with fright. So did Mrs Twiddle.

'Twiddle! Don't do things like that!' she said. 'I've told you before, and –'

Twiddle sat down and closed his eyes. He

thought if he pretended to be asleep, Mrs Twiddle wouldn't go on scolding him. But she did. However, in a few minutes Twiddle really was asleep.

He was awakened by a very cold draught blowing round his neck. He sat up and looked around. The door was wide open again.

'The cat's just come in,' said Mrs Twiddle. 'I expect she found it cold outside today, poor lamb. Would you shut the door, Twiddle?'

Then Twiddle lost his temper. He swooped on the astonished cat, caught tight hold of it, and ran upstairs with it. He pushed it into the spare bedroom, where all the windows were tightly closed, and then slammed and locked the door.

'Now, you just stay there, where you can't get out or in!' said Twiddle. 'Making me open windows and shut doors all the afternoon! Grrrrrrrr!'

The cat settled down in the middle of the eiderdown, purring. Twiddle went downstairs, looking fierce. 'Now, listen to me – that cat stays there all the afternoon, do you hear?'

Mrs Twiddle knew she couldn't do anything with Twiddle when he really was in a temper, so she didn't say anything at all.

Presently there was a peculiar noise from upstairs. The boards creaked loudly, as if someone was walking over the spare-room floor.

'Whatever's that?' said Mrs Twiddle, looking alarmed, and she half-rose to go up to see.

'Sit down,' said Twiddle. 'You know it's the cat. I'm not going to let you go upstairs and let her out. Sit down. She's just walking about.'

'But you can't usually hear cats walk!' cried Mrs Twiddle.

'She's probably stamping around in a temper,' said Twiddle. 'Sit down!'

Soon there was another noise, as if something was falling. Mrs Twiddle leapt up. 'I must go and see what's happening!'

'SIT DOWN!' roared Twiddle. 'It's the cat walking about on the dressing-table, that's all, and knocking over the candlesticks!'

'But the cat never walks on the dressing-table,' said Mrs Twiddle. Still, she sat down, because Twiddle really did look so very fierce.

Presently there was a squeaking noise, and Mrs Twiddle looked up to the ceiling, above which was the spare room. 'What's that?' she said.

'The cat squealing,' said Twiddle, pleased. 'Let it squeal. Do it good. It's got nobody to open and shut doors and windows for it up there and it's angry.'

'But that squeak sounded exactly as if the wardrobe door was being opened,' said Mrs Twiddle, alarmed. 'It always squeaks like that.'

'Well, I daresay your cat can open wardrobe doors as easily as it can open the kitchen door, and make a draught down my neck,' said Twiddle. 'Sit down!'

After that there was a curious slithering sound, and then nothing at all. Mrs Twiddle went on with her knitting. Twiddle fell asleep. But he was awakened once more by a draught blowing down his neck, and when he turned round, there was the door opening wide again – and the cat walking in, purring loudly!

'Puss dear! Clever Puss! How did you get out of the spare room?' said Mrs Twiddle, pleased. 'Twiddle, isn't she clever! How in the world did she manage it?'

Twiddle stared at the cat, astonished and angry. It couldn't get out of the spare room – and yet there is was!

'It must be another cat!' said Twiddle at last. 'Our own must be in the spare room. Why, I locked it in!'

Twiddle went up to the spare room. How strange – the door was still locked! And the windows had been closed – so how could the cat have got out? He unlocked the door and looked in.

The window was wide open! The wardrobe door was wide open, too – and Twiddle's best coat was gone! The drawers of the chest were open, and Mrs Twiddle's best bedcover, which was kept there, was gone. So were the silver candlesticks off the dressing-table, and the clock from the mantelpiece. Oh dear, what could have happened?

Mrs Twiddle heard Twiddle's groan and came hurrying up. When she saw what had happened, she burst into tears.

'A burglar came! He must have climbed up the drain-pipe whilst we were in the kitchen, and he tramped about overhead and opened drawers, and knocked things over, and opened the wardrobe door which squeaks –

and we heard everything – and you said it was the cat! If you hadn't been unkind to the cat, and shut her in here, and said she made all the noise, poor lamb, we'd have shot up to the spare room and caught the burglar at once!'

Twiddle felt very, very uncomfortable. He had to tell the whole story to the police later on, and they tried hard not to laugh.

'I hope you'll never be hard on poor Puss again,' said Mrs Twiddle that evening.

'I wasn't hard on her,' said Twiddle. 'She's hard on me – making me shut doors and –'

'Now, that's enough!' said Mrs Twiddle. 'You've done enough damage for one day, Twiddle, losing your temper. Don't lose it again. Look, take the cat for me a minute. I've got to peep in the oven.'

And will you believe it, poor Twiddle had to nurse the cat the whole evening. She purred so loudly that he couldn't hear the radio properly. What a shame!

Chapter 2

Mr Twiddle and the Boots

Once Mrs Twiddle turned out the landing cupboard, and she found two pairs of Mr Twiddle's old boots. She took them down to the kitchen and looked at them.

'Well, they could really be mended,' she said to herself. 'They want new soles, but that's all. The heels are quite good, and so are the upper parts. In these hard days we mustn't throw old boots away. I'll tell Twiddle to take them to be soled.'

So when Twiddle came in from his walk, he saw the two pairs of old boots on the table. He looked at them in surprise.

'Fancy those old things turning up again!' he said. 'I haven't seen them for years.'

'They must be soled,' said Mrs Twiddle. 'The soles are very bad. Look at them.'

'Yes, so they are,' said Twiddle, looking at the big holes in the soles. 'All right dear – they shall be sold.'

Now Twiddle was making a very great mistake. He thought that Mrs Twiddle meant him to sell the boots. When she said they must be soled, he thought she meant sold. She really meant that the soles must be mended, of course – but he didn't know that.

He wrapped the boots up in brown paper and set off down the road to the shop that

bought old clothes. 'I ought to get a nice lot of money for these boots,' thought Twiddle pleased. 'What shall I buy with the money? I want a new pipe, really. And Mrs Twiddle could do with some boiled sweets. She does like them so much. And the cat could have a kipper. It has behaved quite well lately.'

Mr Twiddle sold the boots and with the money he got, he bought himself a fine new pipe.

He went to the sweet-shop and bought a bag of sweets for Mrs Twiddle. And he bought a kipper for the cat, so Twiddle had no money left by the time he got home.

He put down the sweets on the table. Mrs Twiddle was delighted to see them. 'Oh, thank you,' she said. 'That is kind of you. I thought you hadn't any money left this week.'

'Well, I've just taken the boots to be sold,' said Twiddle. 'The man gave me the money!'

'But, Twiddle, why did the man give you money?' asked Mrs Twiddle, thinking that the cobbler must have gone mad. After all, she always had to pay money to have her shoes mended – it seemed the wrong way about for the man to pay Twiddle!

'Well, boots that are sold bring in money,

don't they?' said Twiddle, thinking that his wife was being very stupid, all of a sudden. 'Look – I got myself a new pipe, too.'

Mrs Twiddle stared at the fine pipe. She simply could not understand how it was that Twiddle had got money for taking boots to be mended!

'And I got a kipper for the cat, too,' said Twiddle. 'Puss, Puss, Puss!'

The cat jumped up at the kipper. Mrs Twiddle really felt in a whirl . . . Sweets for her – a pipe for Twiddle – and a kipper for the cat – all because she had sent Twiddle with two pairs of boots to be mended. Well, well, well!

Someone came to the back door just as Mrs Twiddle was going to ask Twiddle a little bit more about it all. When she came back, Twiddle had gone out into the garden, and she forgot all about the affair until three days later.

Then she remembered the boots. She was just going out and she called to Twiddle. 'Twiddle! Look after the kitchen fire for me. I'll be back soon. I'm going to get the groceries, and I shall call at the boot-shop for your two pairs of boots.'

Twiddle stared at his wife in the greatest surprise. 'Two pairs of boots!' he said. 'That's funny! I've only got two pairs of boots – and one pair is on my feet, and the other is over there waiting to be cleaned.'

'I mean the boots that are being mended,' said Mrs Twiddle.

'But there aren't any being mended,' said Twiddle, wondering if his wife was quite well. 'I tell you my boots are on my feet – and over there. Don't be silly, dear.'

'Twiddle, I'll thank you not to call me silly,' said Mrs Twiddle, offended. 'I know what I'm doing. If you've forgotten that there are boots of yours being mended, I haven't!'

She stalked out down the garden path, leaving Twiddle very puzzled. She went to the boot-shop and asked for Twiddle's boots.

'He brought two pairs here on Monday,' she said. 'They were to be soled, but not heeled. And by the way, did you give Mr Twiddle money when he brought the boots to you? It seemed such a funny thing to me!'

The cobbler looked in surprise at Mrs Twiddle. 'I didn't give Mr Twiddle anything,' he said, 'and I haven't got his boots either. I don't know what you mean.'

'But you must have his boots!' said Mrs Twiddle. 'I gave him two old pairs to bring here to be mended. Oh, please, do look for them! Maybe you've forgotten that he brought them.'

The cobbler looked all round his shop. There were big boots and little ones there, but not Twiddle's. The cobbler shook his head.

'I'm quite certain that Mr Twiddle didn't bring any boots here,' he said. 'He must have taken them to the other cobbler. I feel offended at that, Mrs Twiddle, for you've dealt with me for years!'

He bent over his work quite angry. Mrs Twiddle blushed, for she hated anyone to be angry with her. She went out of the shop, furious with Twiddle, because she thought he had gone with his boots to the other cobbler's and hadn't told her. She hurried home as fast as she could go.

'Twiddle!' she cried, bursting into the kitchen. 'Twiddle! Why did you take your boots to the other cobbler on Monday, instead of to the one we always go to? Now you just tell me that!'

Twiddle really thought his wife had gone mad. Here she was talking about boots again! He thought he had better get her to bed and fetch the doctor. So he put his arm round her and tried to get her to the stairs. Mrs Twiddle was really angry.

'Twiddle! Let go of my arm! What do you mean by saying I must go to bed and see the doctor? It's you who ought to do that! You're losing your memory. You've forgotten already that you took those old pairs of boots to be soled on Monday!'

'Dear me, I haven't forgotten that,' said Twiddle, suddenly remembering. 'I told you I'd taken them, didn't I? And I bought you some boiled sweets out of the money that the man gave me.'

'He didn't give you any money!' cried poor Mrs Twiddle. 'He says he didn't. I asked him. Why do you tell me dreadful stories like that, Twiddle? To think we have been married for thirty years and now you are beginning to tell me stories!'

'I tell you, dear, I took those boots to the old-clothes' shop, and I sold them, just as you told me to,' said Twiddle, quite in despair. 'I don't know why the man said he didn't give me any money, but he did, and I spent it all.'

Mrs Twiddle stared at Twiddle, and suddenly she knew what had happened. She gave a groan that startled Twiddle very much.

'Oh, foolish man! Oh, stupid, ridiculous man! Oh, silly, silly man! I told you those boots were to be soled – s-o-l-e-d, Twiddle – and you went and sold them – s-o-l-d. I wanted you to get new soles put under them – and you go and sell them! Twiddle, will you ever, ever do anything really sensible? No – you never will!'

Chapter 3

Mrs Twiddle Gets Cross

Mr Twiddle sat in his chair reading the newspaper. Mrs Twiddle sat by the fire, knitting. Click, click, click went her needles.

Mr Twiddle sniffed. Mrs Twiddle didn't say anything but she looked at him. He sniffed again.

'Don't,' said Mrs Twiddle. 'Where's your hanky, Twiddle?'

'Don't know,' said Twiddle, and sniffed again.

'But I gave you a clean one this morning!' said Mrs Twiddle. 'It must be in our pocket.'

'Well, it's not,' said Twiddle. 'I've looked. I must have lost it when I went out for a walk. I remember taking it out once, but I don't remember putting it back into my pocket again.'

'Now I shall have to give you another hanky!' groaned Mrs Twiddle. 'Anyone would think I was made of hankies!'

'No, they wouldn't, love,' said Twiddle, looking at his plump little wife.

'Twiddle, I shall have to do something about your hankies,' said Mrs Twiddle, knitting very quickly, as she always did when she was cross. 'You've lost five this week. Five!'

'Oh, no, dear,' said Twiddle.

Oh, yes, Mr Twiddle!' said Mrs Twiddle,

and she rattled her needles loudly. 'Five! It's got to stop. Next time you go out I shall pin your hanky inside your umbrella. Then you won't be able to lose it!'

'But it will be awfully difficult to blow my nose if my hanky is pinned inside my umbrella,' said Twiddle.

'No it won't. You can put your umbrella up and the hanky will unfold and fall down to your nose,' said Mrs Twiddle. 'You won't be able to leave it behind because it will be pinned to your umbrella. When you've used it you can just fold up your umbrella and put it down again.'

'But have I got to put my umbrella up every time I want to blow my nose?' said Twiddle, alarmed.

'Yes,' said Mrs Twiddle. 'Then perhaps you will learn not to lose your hankies.'

She was as good as her word. Next time poor Twiddle went out Mrs Twiddle pinned his hanky firmly to the inside of his big umbrella.

'There!' she said. 'Now you just can't help bringing your hanky home!'

Mr Twiddle went out, hoping that he wouldn't have to blow his nose the whole afternoon. He couldn't bear the idea of putting up his umbrella every time he wanted to use his hanky.

Luckily he didn't want to blow his nose at all. He walked to the paper-shop, and then he went on into the country, meaning to sit on the stile he liked, and read his paper.

He soon came to the stile. He climbed up and opened his newspaper. He hung his umbrella on the top bar of the stile. Then he began to read.

The paper was very interesting. Although Mr Twiddle had read almost exactly the same news in his morning newspaper it seemed just as interesting when he read it the second time. He read for so long that he forgot the time.

When he at last looked at his watch he was alarmed to see that it was almost tea-time.

'Now I shall be late for tea!' he said, and got off the stile in a great hurry. 'Good gracious! I must run.'

So he ran, and just got home as Mrs Twiddle was making the tea. 'Late as usual!' she said. 'Did you have a nice walk? Sit down. Tea is ready.'

Twiddle felt very hot with his hurrying. He

panted. His forehead felt wet with heat, and he felt in his pocket for his hanky. It wasn't there, of course.

So he wiped his forehead with the back of his hand. Mrs Twiddle saw him.

'Oh, Twiddle, where are your manners! Wipe your forehead with your hanky, do!'

'Haven't got it,' said Twiddle, feeling in all his pockets again.

'Well, I pinned it inside your umbrella. Have you forgotten already?' said Mrs Twiddle.

Mr Twiddle got up to get his umbrella. But it wasn't in the hall-stand. How extraordinary. It was always there. But now it wasn't. What had happened to it?

And then, with an awful shock, Twiddle remembered that he had left it behind, hooked to the stile! Yes, he had hooked the handle to the top bar of the stile, with the hanky pinned in it – and he had left them both there! Now what would Mrs Twiddle say?

'Perhaps I could pop upstairs and get another hanky before she notices anything – and then after tea I could see if my umbrella is still on the stile,' thought poor Twiddle.

But there wasn't any time to go and get a

new hanky, because Mrs Twiddle called out impatiently.

'Twiddle! What are you doing out there in the hall? Isn't your hanky in the umbrella?'

'Er – yes, my dear, it is,' said Mr Twiddle, thinking that it certainly must be.

'Well, bring it then,' said Mrs Twiddle. 'You can surely unpin it?'

'Well – er – yes, love,' said Twiddle, wondering how he was to unpin a hanky from an umbrella that wasn't there.

'I suppose your big clumsy hands can't undo the pin!' called Mrs Twiddle, getting annoyed. 'Bring the umbrella here then and

I'll unpin the hanky. The scones are all getting cold. Dear, dear, I never knew such a man!'

Well, that was worse than ever. How could he bring in an umbrella that wasn't there?

'The umbrella isn't here,' called Mr Twiddle.

'Why not?' called back Mrs Twiddle, puzzled.

'Well, I must have left it on the stile,' said Mr Twiddle, not daring to go back into the kitchen. But Mrs Twiddle at once popped out into the hall.

'What! You've lost your umbrella now! You just put on your hat and go straight back to the stile and get it. Anyone might take it!'

So poor Twiddle had to leave his nice tea and go hurrying off to the stile. He was in such a flurry that he didn't notice Mr Jinks hurrying in the opposite direction, carrying his umbrella with him. Mr Jinks had passed by the stile and had seen the umbrella. He knew it was Mr Twiddle's and now he was hurrying to take it back.

Twiddle didn't hear him calling. He just went panting on – and when he came to the stile, the umbrella wasn't there, of course.

So back went poor Twiddle, very much afraid that Mrs Twiddle would have a great deal to say to him that evening. He was very glad indeed when he saw his umbrella standing in the hall again!

'Mr Jinks brought it back,' said Mrs Twiddle. 'I gave him your scones to eat, in return for his kindness! But you can have bread and jam.'

Now the next day Twiddle put on his coat to go out, and once more took his umbrella, which had his hanky still pinned inside. But Mrs Twiddle called him before he went out.

'Twiddle! Come here a minute. Are you taking your hanky and your umbrella?'

'Yes, love,' said Twiddle.

'Well, just to make sure you don't lose your umbrella again, I'm going to tie it to your coat-sleeve with thread,' said Mrs Twiddle. 'Then, even if you do put it down and forget it, it will hang on to your sleeve, so you can't leave it behind. There now – that's tightly tied on, your hanky is pinned to your umbrella – and your umbrella is tied to your coat-sleeve – you can't possibly lose either of them now!'

Mr Twiddle didn't at all like all this pinning and tying, but he didn't dare argue about it.

Mrs Twiddle was so much better at arguing than he was. So he set off, looking rather gloomy.

He thought he would go and look in at his old friend, Mr Peto's. Mr Peto had five children, and it was always a jolly house to go to. So he arrived at Mr Peto's to find him playing an exciting game of rounders with the five boys and girls.

Now Mr Twiddle loved rounders. He loved hitting out at the ball, and he liked trying to get somebody out. So he joined in the game too.

Soon he was feeling very hot, for he had on his coat. 'Take off your coat, man, for goodness' sake!' said Mr Peto, who had nothing on but shorts and a vest.

So Mr Twiddle took off his coat and set it and the umbrella over the bough of a tree. Then he joined in the game. The sun came out and everyone got very hot.

'Lemonade, lemonade!' cried Mr Peto, when the game was finished. 'And ice-creams! Come on down to the village shop, all of you, and we'll drink lemonade and have ice-creams.'

Mr Twiddle liked lemonade and ice-cream too, so he went along, and he paid for a pink ice-cream for everyone. The children thought he was very kind.

Mr Twiddle suddenly heard the village clock strike one. He jumped up. 'My gracious! I said I'd be home at half-past twelve. I must fly. Goodbye!'

Off he went, thinking that it was very funny the way the time went when you were playing games. He came in at the door of his house, feeling rather late and flustered.

'Late again,' said Mrs Twiddle. 'How hot you are! I hope you won't get a chill.'

'A-tish-o!' said Twiddle, feeling for his hanky. It wasn't there, of course.

'Twiddle, you know your hanky is pinned to your umbrella,' said Mrs Twiddle, crossly. 'Go and get it.'

Twiddle went out to the hall to get it. His umbrella was not there.

'Now, don't tell me your umbrella isn't there, Twiddle!' called his wife. 'I tied it to your coat, so that you couldn't leave it behind. Look for your coat, then for your umbrella, then inside for your hanky.'

'Well, my coat isn't here,' said Twiddle, desperately, 'nor my umbrella, nor my hanky.'

Mrs Twiddle came out into the hall in astonishment. 'Well, where is your coat, then?' she said. Twiddle suddenly remembered.

'Well – dear me – yes, I must have left it hanging over the branch of the tree in Mr Peto's garden,' he said. 'I was hot and I took it off. So the umbrella is there, too – and the hanky, of course.

Mrs Twiddle stared at him. 'Are you doing all this on purpose, Twiddle?' she asked sternly. 'I suppose if I pin your coat to your vest you will come home without that too! You are a very annoying man. I shall not

speak to you for the rest of the day.'

This was the kind of punishment that Twiddle really enjoyed, because he thought that Mrs Twiddle spoke far too much. But he pretended to look very sad. After his dinner, Mr Peto brought back his coat, umbrella, and hanky and Mr Twiddle thanked him very much.

'If you want to come to tea, you'd better come today,' he said to Mr Peto, 'because Mrs Twiddle isn't in a speaking mood, and we could have a nice quiet time.'

But, oh dear, Mrs Twiddle overheard what he said, and that was the end of a nice quiet time! Poor Twiddle, he does get himself into trouble, doesn't he?

Chapter 4

Mr Twiddle and the Shears

'Twiddle!' called Mrs Twiddle. 'Are you going down into the town today?'

Twiddle put down his newspaper and groaned. He knew what that question meant. It meant that Mrs Twiddle had a whole lot of shopping for him to do. But for once he was mistaken. She didn't want any shopping done, she only wanted something taken to be sharpened.

'It's the garden shears,' she said. 'They are so very blunt that I can't cut the edges of the grass with them. Could you take them to be mended?'

Well, as the shop that mended such things as shears stood just beside the river, where Mr Twiddle loved to watch the passing ships, he was quite pleased to go. 'Yes, I'll go down into the town, now,' he said. 'If I go now I can watch the twelve o'clock ship passing under the bridge.'

He was very pleased about that. He liked watching the ship, especially when it was crammed full of people. They all waved to him and that made Twiddle feel very important.

He folded up his paper, put it in his chair ready for when he came home, and went to get his hat and stick. He set off happily.

It was almost twelve o'clock when he got to the bridge. There came the ship, flags flying, and a band playing – lovely!

Everyone waved to Mr Twiddle and he waved back happily with his hat. Really, he might be a king, the way he felt when he saw hundreds of people waving like that!

The ship passed by. Mr Twiddle put on his hat again and went into the ironmonger's shop. 'Yes, sir? What can I do for you? asked the boy behind the counter.

'I want some garden shears mended,' said Mr Twiddle.

'Shall I fetch them, sir?' asked the boy.

'No, I've –' began Mr Twiddle, and then he

stopped. Dear me – where were the shears? He hadn't got them with him! What had he done with them?

'Er – I must have left them somewhere,' said Twiddle, and hurried out of the shop. Yes – he had left them at home! He rushed back, and Mrs Twiddle met him at the door.

'You're in nice time for dinner, Twiddle,' she said, pleased. 'When did they say they would have the shears mended? Today?'

'Well, er – you see – the fact is, I didn't take them,' said Twiddle, going rather red. 'I quite forgot them, dear. There they are, on the hall-table.'

'Really, Twiddle! You do some silly things, I

know – but fancy going off to ask for shears to be mended, and leaving them behind all the time!' said Mrs Twiddle, vexed. 'It's too bad of you.'

'Yes, it is,' said Twiddle. 'I'll take them this afternoon.'

So, after he had had his dinner, he got his hat and his stick. 'Mind you take the shears, too!' said Mrs Twiddle, calling from the kitchen.

'I've got them under my arm,' said Twiddle. 'Don't worry!'

Off he went with the shears. It was a lovely day and soon he overtook his old friend Mr Wander. Mr Wander was a great walker, and knew all the little highways and byways of the countryside.

'Where are you going?' he asked Twiddle.

'Nowhere particular,' said Twiddle. 'Just taking these shears along, that's all. I'll come with you a little way, it's such a nice afternoon.

Well, Twiddle and Wander talked and walked and really enjoyed each other's company. When at last Twiddle found himself back at his front gate, he beamed at Wander and shook him warmly by the hand. 'It's a long time since I enjoyed a walk and a talk so much!' he said, and indoors he went.

Mrs Twiddle came to meet him. 'Oh, Twiddle – how lovely! You've waited for the shears to be sharpened and brought them home for me. That is nice of you!'

Twiddle stared down at the shears in horror. Gracious! He had carried them all the way there and back and hadn't even gone into the shop! They were as blunt as when he had set off with them.

It was very, very difficult to explain this to Mrs Twiddle. She kept saying, 'But how could you carry the shears under your arm all that way and never once think of getting them sharpened?' Mr Twiddle felt very foolish and could hardly eat any tea at all.

'Now, tomorrow morning you're to go straight to the shop with those shears, and you're to wait there till they're done,' said Mrs Twiddle. 'First you go without them, then you take them all the way there and back and don't have them sharpened – now you just see that you wait for them!'

So the next morning poor Twiddle had no time to read his paper. He had to set off at once with the shears. Oh dear – suppose the shop couldn't do them till the afternoon? What about his dinner? He would have to go without it if he waited for the shears!

He arrived safely at the shop and was glad to see that the shears were still under his arm. Good! Now to ask the boy when they could be done.

'Yes? Brought the shears this time, I see,' said the boy with a grin. 'You want them sharpened, I suppose, sir?'

'Yes, please,' said Twiddle. 'When can you do them? I'm – er – well, I'm in a bit of a hurry.'

'Can't do them before two o'clock, sir,' said the boy, looking at a list of work to be done. 'Very sorry.'

Mr Twiddle groaned. He would certainly not get home for dinner, then, because he had promised his wife to wait for the shears. 'All right,' he said. 'I'll wait for them.'

He sat down in the shop, and wished he hadn't left his newspaper at home. Then, after a while, he remembered that the eleven o'clock ship would soon be along. He cheered up a bit. He could go and watch that, and the twelve o'clock one, too – and the one o'clock – yes, and he could see the two o'clock one go by as well, just before he collected the shears. Well, well, it wasn't often that he had the chance of watching four ships in one day.

He went off to wait for the eleven o'clock ship. He sat in the sun and snoozed, and most unfortunately missed the ship when it went by. Never mind, he could see the twelve o'clock.

He did, and everyone waved like mad again. Mr Twiddle waved back so madly that he almost dropped his hat in the water.

At half-past twelve he began to feel very hungry. He considered what to do. He couldn't go home to his dinner because Mrs Twiddle would be very angry to see him

coming home again without the shears. But, if he had enough money in his pocket, he could go and have a nice dinner in the little inn near-by, the one that faced on to the river.

'Then I can watch the boats go by all the time,' he thought happily. 'Really, this day is turning out to be quite a nice one for me, after all.'

He went to the shop to find out how much the shears would be when they were sharpened. Then he would know how much money he would be able to spend on his dinner. The boy was still there, behind the counter.

'Your shears aren't ready yet, sir,' he said, 'I said two o'clock, you know.'

'Yes, I know,' said Mr Twiddle. 'I just came in to find out how much they will be when they are done.'

'Three pounds fifty, sir,' said the boy.

'Thank you,' said Twiddle. 'I'll be in at two o'clock to fetch them. I may as well pay for them now, then I can just take the shears and go, when I come in after dinner.'

He paid the three pounds fifty and went out. Now he could spend the rest of his money on his dinner. He had five pounds. He could get a nice meal at the inn for that.

He watched the one o'clock ship go by and then went to get his dinner. It was lovely to sit in the window of the inn, eating cold meat and salad, and be able to watch the ships and barges go by at the same time.

He waited for the two o'clock ship to pass, and then he paid his bill, and walked back to the ironmonger's shop. He went in.

There was nobody there! The boy was lazy and never came back from his dinner at the right time. Bother him!

Twiddle saw a long parcel lying at one end of the counter. It had a ticket on it. Twiddle looked at it, feeling sure that it was his shears. The ticket said three pounds fifty.

'Three pounds fifty – yes, this is my parcel,' he said, pleased. 'Well, as I've paid my bill I don't see why I can't collect these shears and go. It's not my fault that the boy is so late back from his dinner.'

So he put the parcel under his arm and off he went. Mrs Twiddle was out in the garden, trying to cut the grass-edges with an old pair of shears. She was very pleased to see him.

'Ah, good!' she said. 'You've brought them back at last – sharpened this time, I hope!

How much were they?'

'Three pounds fifty,' said Twiddle, and Mrs Twiddle tut-tutted and said that was a dreadful price. She tore the paper off – and then gave a scream.

'Twiddle! What's this? It's a saw! A saw! Do you mean to tell me you took our saw to be sharpened instead of the shears? Well, really, *really*! I don't know what to say to you, honestly I don't.'

All the same, she said a lot, and Twiddle had to listen. He was puzzled. Had he taken the saw instead of the shears? No – he knew he hadn't. Then he had taken somebody else's parcel instead of his own. What a tiresome nuisance.

'Oh – so that's the next silly thing you did, is it?' said Mrs Twiddle. 'Well, I'll give you one more chance of being silly – you can just take this saw back to the shop straight away and get the shears instead!'

So off went poor Mr Twiddle once more. He came to the shop and told the boy what had happened.

'I've brought back the saw, so can I take my shears now?' he asked.

'Oh, my!' said the boy. 'I must have given them to the other customer, when he came for his saw. They were wrapped up, too, you see. He lives at Romer Green, five miles away.'

Well, well, well! – that was too much for Mr Twiddle altogether. He look desperately round the shop. He saw a pair of brand-new shears hanging there.

'I'll buy these,' he said. 'Give them to me now. I'll come in and pay for them tomorrow.'

And he went off home with a new pair of shears for Mrs Twiddle – but whether she'll be pleased or not about that I really don't know. Twiddle does really do some peculiar things, doesn't he?

Chapter 5

Mrs Twiddle Is Very Cross

One day Mrs Twiddle had a great deal to do, and when she had to rush here and there, she was not very good-tempered.

Usually Mr Twiddle kept out of her way then. If he didn't he would be sent on this errand and that and kept very busy, too. He would be scolded if he forgot anything and he didn't like that.

'Twiddle! Put down your paper and go and answer the door!' cried Mrs Twiddle, rolling out some pastry with her rolling-pin.

'Twiddle! The fire is going down! Put some coal on it. Really, why you can't see for yourself that the fire is almost out. I cannot think!

Twiddle! You look even stupider than

usual! Why don't you do something to help me!'

Poor Twiddle. He put down his paper. He ran here and there. He did his best to help.

Mrs Twiddle went to the larder to get the tin of sugar. She screwed up her nose in disgust.

'Bother! The fish has gone bad. Twiddle, where are you? Bless the man, he's gone and put his hat on! Twiddle, you don't think you are going out, do you? Just when I'm so busy and want your help, too. And your best hat! Whatever makes you think I'll let you go out wearing your best Sunday hat on a busy morning like this? You must be mad.'

'No, I'm not,' said Twiddle. 'I want to go and call on old Mrs Jenks to see how she is, and my old hat really wanted cleaning.'

'What! Call on old Mrs Jenks when I want you here! Twiddle, you are enough to drive anyone mad. Now, quick – take this bad fish and put it into the dustbin, and take off that best hat and put it back on the top shelf of the wardrobe. Hurry now!'

Twiddle sighed and tried to hurry. He took off his best hat. Mrs Twiddle pushed the dish of bad fish into his hand. He turned to go out of doors to the dustbin.

'If only I could have slipped out when she wasn't looking!' thought Mr Twiddle, as he took off the dustbin lid. He put in his best hat and slapped the lid on again. Then he went indoors.

He ran upstairs and put the dish of bad fish on the shelf in the wardrobe, where all the hats were kept. He was so busy thinking of how unlucky he was that morning that he didn't notice what he was doing at all. That was exactly like Mr Twiddle – the dearest, kindest old thing, but oh, the silly things he did!

'Now, Twiddle, go and sweep out the yard,' said Mrs Twiddle. 'It's full of rubbish. Put it into the dustbin when you've finished.'

Twiddle swept out the yard. He shovelled up the rubbish and popped it into the dustbin, all on top of his best hat. But he didn't know that.

Twiddle was glad when that day was over and he could go up to bed. He sank into his bed with a sigh and shut his eyes at once. But it wasn't long before Mrs Twiddle sat up in bed and sniffed hard.

'What's the matter?' asked Twiddle, sleepily. 'Are you starting a cold, sniffing like that?'

'I can smell a smell,' said Mrs Twiddle. 'An awful smell.'

'Well, never mind,' said Twiddle. 'Let it be. It won't hurt you. I can't smell a thing.'

'Twiddle, sit up and sniff,' said Mrs Twiddle, and she gave him a pinch. 'It's a terrible smell.'

Twiddle groaned. He sat up and sniffed – and sure enough there really was a most peculiar and horrible smell in the bedroom. Whatever could it be?

'It's like fish,' said Mrs Twiddle.

'Impossible,' said Twiddle.

'I know,' said Mrs Twiddle. 'But it's exactly like very bad fish – very bad fish indeed. How very extraordinary!'

'Most,' said Twiddle, and lay down again. But Mrs Twiddle wasn't going to have that. No – that smell had got to be found. No doubt about that!

'Get up and see if you can find where the smell is coming from,' said Mrs Twiddle. So Twiddle got out of bed and sniffed hard again. It seemed to come from the wardrobe. He went over to it. He opened the door – and at once the smell came out, ten times stronger!

'Oooof!' said Mrs Twiddle. 'It must be something the cat's brought in! How simply disgusting! Twiddle, look in the wardrobe.'

Twiddle looked. The smell seemed to come from the top shelf where the hats were kept. He stood on a chair and looked – and there, among the hats, was the dish of bad fish!

Twiddle stared at it in horror. How in the world could he have been so stupid as to put it there! He stood still for such a long time that Mrs Twiddle grew impatient.

'What's the matter, Twiddle? What's in the wardrobe?'

'Fish,' said Twiddle in a small voice.

'Fish!' said Mrs Twiddle, not at all believing him. 'Don't be silly. Fish couldn't get into the wardrobe.'

'It is fish,' said Twiddle. 'I'll take it downstairs and put it into the dustbin. Most extraordinary thing. Never heard of such a thing in my life. Can't think what the cat's been up to, to take fish into the wardrobe.'

'Nor can I,' said Mrs Twiddle, angry and puzzled. 'Twiddle, it's cold tonight. Just put your best hat on, and your coat. I sent your old hat to be cleaned this afternoon.'

Twiddle looked for his best hat. It wasn't there.

'It's not there,' he said.

'It must be,' said Mrs Twiddle, impatiently. 'You put it there yourself this morning. Find it at once, or I'll come and look for it!'

Twiddle turned pale. He suddenly knew what had happened. He must have put his best hat into the dustbin – and put the bad fish into the wardrobe. Mrs Twiddle could wait no longer. She jumped out of bed and went to find Twiddle's hat.

She saw the dish of fish. She stared at
Twiddle, and he stared back, red in the face
now, instead of white! Poor Twiddle!

'Twiddle! The cat may be clever enough to
carry fish to the wardrobe – but not on a dish!
You must have put it there! Dreaming as
usual! But oh, Twiddle, don't tell me you put
that lovely best hat of yours into the dustbin?'

Twiddle didn't tell her. She knew! He went
downstairs with the bad fish, and made his
way out into the yard. The cat followed him,
sniffing eagerly at the fish. Twiddle put the
fish into the dustbin, and then looked for his
hat. It was there, covered with rubbish, tea-
leaves – and now fish!

Twiddle put the lid on the dustbin again. He didn't know that the cat had jumped in after the fish, and was shut in. He went sadly back to the bedroom holding his hat in his hand. How it smelt!

Mrs Twiddle said a lot to him, and he had to listen. It was a long time before he went to sleep. When he woke up he remembered what had happened.

'I must be very, very careful today,' he thought. 'I'll do nothing to make Mrs Twiddle angry at all!'

So he was as good as he could be and Mrs Twiddle was pleased – until she discovered the cat shut in the dustbin!

'So this is why you've been so good and quiet!' she scolded. 'You'd shut the poor cat in the dustbin! You bad man! Twiddle, I've a good mind to shut you up in the dustbin too!'

She looked so fierce that Twiddle snatched a hat from the hallstand, and fled. It wasn't until he was a mile away that he found he had taken Mrs Twiddle's old hat by mistake.

No wonder everyone laughed when he went by! He really is a funny fellow, isn't he?

Chapter 6

Mr Twiddle Lets the Cat In

'Twiddle, dear, let the cat out, will you?' said Mrs Twiddle, busily knitting in her chair by the fire.

'I don't know why you can't teach that cat to open the doors,' grumbled Mr Twiddle, getting up. 'You always say she's so very, very clever – and yet she has never learnt a simple thing like that!'

'Well, she's very sharp, the way she goes and sits by the door whenever she wants to come in or out,' said Mrs Twiddle. 'Do hurry, Twiddle.'

'I shall keep the cat waiting if I like,' said Mr Twiddle who had never been able to like his wife's cat. He stopped to take something out of a drawer. The cat miaowed.

'Don't call me names!' said Twiddle. 'You're a most annoying creature. When you're out you want to come in, and when you're in, you want to go out. I know you! You just want to go and have a chat with the cat next door, so you make me get up and let you out – and then when you find the cat next door isn't there, you'll want me to get up and let you in. You're a nuisance.'

'Miaow!' said the cat, and began to wash herself. Mr Twiddle opened the door, but the cat went on washing herself.

'Look at that now!' said Twiddle, exasperated. 'Asking to go out and she doesn't want to after all! All right, I'll shut the door, Puss, and next time you want to go out you can *wait*!'

He shut the door, but before it was quite closed the cat slipped out like a shadow, and the tip of her tail was caught in the door. She gave such an anguished yowl that Mrs Twiddle leapt out of her chair.

'Twiddle! How cruel you are! You shut the cat in the door!'

'I did not,' said Twiddle, a little scared himself by the cat's dreadful yowl. 'She slid out as I was shutting the door and the tip of her tail got pinched, that's all. Serve her right.'

'I will not have you talk like that,' said Mrs Twiddle, getting all upset, and dropping a stitch in her knitting.

'Well, we'll not talk any more about it,' said Twiddle, sitting down with his newspaper again. 'There's no more to be said.'

But there was, because Mrs Twiddle had a great deal to say. By the time she had finished Mr Twiddle was certain that he was the cruellest man in the world, and that he had upset his wife enough to make her feel quite ill, and had half-killed the poor, dear cat.

'And now I suppose you won't get her in tonight,' said Mrs Twiddle, a tear dropping on to her knitting. 'You'll make her stay out in the cold.'

'I will get her in,' said kind-hearted Mr Twiddle, who really couldn't bear to see his wife upset. 'I'm sorry I pinched her tail. I promise you I'll get her in tonight.'

'Thank you, Twiddle,' said Mrs Twiddle in a small voice, and smiled at him. After that he read his newspaper in peace, and forgot all about the cat till Mrs Twiddle said it really was time for bed. She put away her knitting and got up.

'You'll get the cat in, dear, won't you?' she said.

'Oh dear me, the cat, yes, I'll get her in,' said Twiddle. 'You go on up.'

'Open the back door, dear, and she'll come in there and go straight to her basket by the fire,' said Mrs Twiddle. 'There are mice there, and I like her to sleep there now instead of here in the kitchen.'

'Right,' said Twiddle, and opened the door for Mrs Twiddle to go upstairs. Then he yawned, made up the fire for the night, and wound up the clock. Then he went out of the kitchen into the scullery and opened the door.

No cat came sliding in by his legs. He called loudly. 'Puss, Puss, Puss! Come along! Puss, Puss!'

No Puss came. Mr Twiddle waited for about three minutes, till he felt rather cold. Then he called again, rather impatiently.

'Puss! PUSS! Don't you hear me? Come along in at once.'

No cat appeared. Mr Twiddle began to wish he hadn't promised to let her in that night.

Suppose the cat kept him standing there for an hour? It would be just like her. She was probably hiding in a bush just outside, laughing to herself to see him standing there waiting. Twiddle felt angry.

Then an idea came to him. He would tempt the cat in. He went to the larder and found the fish for breakfast, three nice herrings. He took one, wrapped it up in a newspaper and then laid it on the mat just inside the scullery door. Then he went back to the warm kitchen and sat down with his paper again, to wait for the cat to come in. He was sure he would hear the rustling of the paper, as the cat tried to get at the herring.

Then he meant to hop up, shut the door and put the fish back into the larder! Such a nice, simple plan, thought Mr Twiddle. As indeed it was.

Unfortunately, Mr Twiddle fell sound asleep as soon as he got back into his chair. He didn't hear the cat come in and fiddle at the paper round the fish. He didn't hear the next-door cat come in, too, and get excited about the herring. He didn't even hear the ginger cat across the road walk in, or the big tabby from the bottom of the garden.

Mrs Twiddle's cat was angry to think she might have to share the herring with the others. She spat and hissed at them. Then in walked Black Tom, the biggest cat in the town, and all the others made way for him.

Black Tom began to tear at the paper. The other cats came closer. He hit out at them. The tabby hit back, spitting and snarling. Then, quite suddenly, all the cats exploded together into one big hiss of anger.

The noise awoke Mr Twiddle. He sat up and remembered his plan of getting the cat indoors. She's there now, he thought to himself. How clever I am! I'll just pop the fish back into the larder, and shut the scullery door. 'Hi, Puss, is that you?'

All five cats heard his voice and became quiet. They hid in different places as he came out into the dark scullery. He groped about for the fish and found it on the floor, its paper almost off. He popped it into the larder, and spoke to the cat.

'Now you settle down and go to sleep, Puss! No more going in and out tonight!'

He went back into the kitchen. Unfortunately, he had left the larder door open, and the cats soon found this out. As

soon as Twiddle was safely upstairs in bed, Black Tom led the way to the fish-smell in the larder. The parcel of herrings was dragged down with a thud. A small dish came with it and broke on the floor. The cats spat at one another.

Mrs Twiddle awoke with a jump, when the dish broke. She sat up in bed and listened. She couldn't make out what the noise downstairs was at all.

She clutched poor Twiddle and woke him up with a start. 'Twiddle! It's burglars! They're downstairs.'

Twiddle had often been awakened by Mrs Twiddle and told there were burglars. But there never had been and he was getting tired of going downstairs for nothing. He turned over and settled himself comfortably again.

'Rubbish!' he said, sleepily. 'You're imagining things as usual.'

Pssssssssssssst! went the cats, and one of them gave a frightful howl. Mr Twiddle groaned in fright.

'Twiddle! You simply must go down and see what it is!' whispered Mrs Twiddle. Twiddle didn't want to in the least. But he had to pretend to be brave even if he didn't feel it, so down he went, with a poker in his hand.

The noise came from the scullery. Mr Twiddle switched on the light suddenly, and then stood still in horror at the scene. The place was full of cats! They chewed and hissed, gnawed and spat! Mr Twiddle went suddenly mad with rage.

He leapt at them, dealing out swipes with his bare hand, for even in his rage he felt he couldn't use the poker. The cats began to yowl and snarl, almost falling over one another, trying to get away from the angry man.

'Brrrrr! That's for you! Grrrrrr! Take that. How dare you come into my house! Out of my way, out of my way! I'll teach you to come here in the middle of the night!'

Mrs Twiddle, trembling upstairs, felt certain that Mr Twiddle must be dealing with at least five dangerous burglars. How brave of him! How marvellous he was! Then she heard the scullery door open and then shut again with a bang.

After that Mr Twiddle came upstairs, panting and angry. Mrs Twiddle greeted him with open arms.

'Twiddle, dear! How brave you are! Are you hurt? How many were there?'

'Five at least,' said Twiddle, 'probably seven or eight. Anyway, I've dealt with them and sent them all flying.'

'I think you're marvellous,' said Mrs Twiddle, still thinking that Mr Twiddle had fought burglars. Mr Twiddle was pleased and surprised at his wife's admiration.

'I went for them like anything,' he said. 'You should have seen them rush out of the scullery door, tails out behind them!'

Mrs Twiddle was astonished. 'Tails?' she said. 'Did you say tails? How could they have tails?'

'Well, don't cats generally have tails?' said Mr Twiddle.

'Cats! Were they cats? I thought they were burglars!' cried Mrs Twiddle.

'Of course they were cats,' said Mr Twiddle crossly. 'I suppose that stupid animal of yours brought them all in. They've eaten practically everything in the larder.'

'Oh! How wicked! How dreadful!' cried Mrs Twiddle. 'Oh, Twiddle, I do hope you gave our puss a scolding, too, and sent her out. I hope you didn't let her in again.'

'I did not,' said Mr Twiddle. 'I had great pleasure in scolding her. Now perhaps you won't make me keep getting up to go and let her in and out.'

'I certainly won't,' said Mrs Twiddle, very angry indeed to think that her petted, spoilt cat should actually have dared to fill the scullery with her friends and raid the larder.

Well, well, well! Puss could certainly stay out all night.

Twiddle fell asleep and snored a little. Mrs Twiddle lay and thought about the cats. Then she suddenly sat up and poked Twiddle hard.

'Twiddle! There's something I want to know. Who left the larder door open, so that the cats got in?'

But Twiddle was not going to answer questions like that. Not he! He snored a little louder, and made no movement at all. Leave that till the morning! Perhaps Mrs Twiddle would forget about it by then.

But she won't! It's quite certain she will remember to ask Twiddle that question, and a lot more besides. Poor Twiddle – he does get himself into trouble, doesn't he?

Chapter 7

Mr Twiddle's Meat Pie

'My sister Harriet has asked us to go and see her tomorrow, Twiddle dear,' said Mrs Twiddle. 'Won't that be nice?'

Twiddle didn't think it would be at all nice. He didn't like Harriet. She was always remembering silly things he had done, and reminding him of them. It wouldn't be so bad if Harriet did silly things herself, then he could do some remembering, too. But she never did anything silly.

'Well,' said Twiddle, 'well – do you think we ought to go when food is so expensive? We shall have to have dinner there, you know.'

'How nice of you to think of such a thing,' said Mrs Twiddle, pleased. 'Quite right – food is expensive just now – so you can go out this afternoon and buy a meat pie from the butcher's shop. You won't have to stand in the queue for more than an hour, I should think.'

Twiddle wished he hadn't said anything about food or dinner. Now he would have to take a basket, go out in the rain and hope the meat pies wouldn't be all sold by the time he got his turn.

But he had to go. 'Put on your mac and your boots,' said Mrs Twiddle. 'And take an umbrella. And remember to put it up, Twiddle. Last time you went out in the rain with your umbrella you forgot to put it up.'

'All right, all right,' said Twiddle. He put on his mac and his boots, took his umbrella and a basket, and out he walked. He didn't have to stand very long in the queue after all, and he got a fine big meat pie, piping hot and smelling most delicious. He felt quite pleased with himself.

When he got home, Mrs Twiddle, who was upstairs, shouted down to him: 'Stand your umbrella in the porch outside to dry. Put your boots in the boot-cupboard, and put the meat pie in the larder.'

Well, Mr Twiddle put all the things away,

but, unfortunately, he made a little mistake. He stood his umbrella in the porch outside all right, but he was rather dreamy when he took his boots off, and he put them on the shelf in the larder instead of in the boot cupboard.

Then he put the meat pie into the boot cupboard and shut the door. He whistled a little tune, went into the kitchen, sat down and took up the newspaper. Now, perhaps he could have a little rest.

Mrs Twiddle hurried down, poked the fire, found her knitting, and sat down, too. She chattered away to Twiddle, who said, 'Ooom, ooom,' now and then, and went on reading his newspaper.

The cat came into the kitchen and mewed.

'What do you want, Pussy?' said Mrs Twiddle. 'Do you want a drink? Twiddle, give the cat some milk.'

'It doesn't want a drink,' said Twiddle, who hated to be disturbed by the cat. 'It's just mewing. It doesn't want a drink every time it mews.'

'Give it some milk, Twiddle,' said Mrs Twiddle; and Mr Twiddle did. The cat drank it. It went out into the hall and smelt round

about the boot cupboard. It came back and mewed again. It could smell the pie in the cupboard, and it felt astonished and excited.

'See if the cat wants to go out-of-doors, Twiddle,' said Mrs Twiddle.

'It doesn't,' said Twiddle. 'It's just being a nuisance. Go away, Puss. I want to read my paper.'

'Let the cat out, Twiddle,' said Mrs Twiddle; and Mr Twiddle did. But it came in again almost at once, jumping through the window very near to Twiddle's head. It made him jump, and he was annoyed with the cat.

'Can't you make up your mind what you

want?' he said to it, fiercely. 'You don't seem to know if you're coming or going. Sit down and wash yourself.'

The cat didn't. It gave Twiddle a rude stare, then went into the hall again. It smelt round the boot cupboard, feeling more and more excited. Either there was a boot there that smelt exactly like a meat pie or, by some surprising chance, there really was a pie inside. The cat couldn't open the cupboard, but it tried to, scraping away at the edge with its claws.

Mrs Twiddle heard it. She wondered what the cat wanted. Perhaps there was a mouse in the hall. 'Twiddle,' she said, 'see what the cat wants, will you? It's making such a noise out there.'

'It doesn't want anything,' said Twiddle, annoyed. 'It's just being tiresome. It often is.'

'Go and see what the cat wants,' said Mrs Twiddle; and Twiddle went. He watched the cat nosing round the boot cupboard. He saw a fine way of getting rid of the cat for the whole afternoon. He'd shut it in the boot-cupboard and let it sniff round for mice there and be happy.

So Mr Twiddle opened the cupboard door,

shot the cat in quickly, and closed the door again. Then he went back to his chair and took up his newspaper.

The cat soon found the pie. It was still in its paper bag, so it had to tear the paper open. It pulled the pie around among the boots, and had a glorious time. Mrs Twiddle was surprised to hear it making such a noise in the cupboard.

'What can the cat be doing?' she said.

'Ooom?' said Mr Twiddle, not taking any notice.

'It seems to be tearing paper,' said Mrs Twiddle.

'Let it,' said Twiddle, annoyed.

The cat lost a bit of pie down a boot and scrabbled after it. 'Good gracious, you haven't shut the poor cat in the boot cupboard, have you?' said Mrs Twiddle.

'Hunting for mice, I expect,' said Twiddle, feeling that at any moment he would have to get up again and let the cat out.

'That reminds me,' said Mrs Twiddle. 'What sort of meat pie did you get? Was it nice and fresh? Was it a nice big one?'

'A beauty,' said Twiddle.

'I think I'll have a look at it,' said Mrs

Twiddle. 'If it's on the small side we'd better take a pound of sausages with us, too.'

'I tell you it's a nice big one,' said Twiddle, in alarm, thinking that he would now be told to go out and buy sausages. Mrs Twiddle got up and went to the larder. She opened the door – and the very first thing she saw was a pair of dirty boots standing on the shelf. She gave a squeal.

'Gracious! What's this?'

'What's what?' said Twiddle.

'This!' said Mrs Twiddle, indignantly, and she held up the boots. 'On my clean shelf, in my clean larder! What do you mean by it, Twiddle? Have you gone mad?'

Twiddle stared at the boots. He must have put them there without thinking. 'Er – er – sorry, dear,' he said. 'It was a mistake.'

'I should think it was,' said Mrs Twiddle, throwing the boots on to the floor. 'Now, where's that meat pie? I can't see it!'

No meat pie was there. Mrs Twiddle turned to Twiddle and scolded him. 'Where did you put the pie? Didn't I tell you to put it here? Have you taken it to your bedroom? Have you left it in the porch?'

Mr Twiddle couldn't remember. 'I'll go

and look,' he said. Mrs Twiddle pointed to his boots.

'Put them into the boot cupboard as you go by,' she said. Twiddle picked them up. He went to the boot cupboard and opened it. The cat shot out at once, looking remarkably fat. A curious smell came from the cupboard – rather tasty and rich. Mr Twiddle smelt it – and a peculiar look came over his face.

He must have put the meat pie into the boot cupboard instead of his boots. And he had shut the cat in there too – so there wouldn't be any meat pie left. It was all very tiresome. What could he do about it?

'Have you found that meat pie yet?' called Mrs Twiddle. 'I can't see it anywhere.'

'Well, dear,' said Mr Twiddle, going into the kitchen, trying to smile, 'well, dear, it's like this – you see – well, what I did was – er, er – it's very funny really.'

Mrs Twiddle looked at him and a cold stare came over her face. 'What have you done now, Twiddle?' she said. 'Don't tell me you put the meat pie into the boot cupboard – and shut the cat in there too!'

'Well – I won't tell you if you'd rather I didn't,' said Twiddle, backing out of the kitchen. 'But I must have done something like that – quite by mistake, of course – and how was I to know the cat was smelling it? Well, I'll go out and get another.'

He went out – but he didn't get another, because they were all sold out. Mrs Twiddle was cross.

'Now we shan't be able to go and see Harriet,' she said. 'I'm not going unless I take something with me – and they don't make pies tomorrow. We can't go. What a pity!'

'Well!' thought Twiddle, sitting down in his chair and picking up his paper again, 'that's a bit of good luck anyway! Shan't see Harriet tomorrow after all. That is a bit of good luck.

And it looks as if I'll be able to read my paper in peace now.'

The cat came into the kitchen, mewing. 'Poor creature!' said Mrs Twiddle. 'All that meat pie has made it feel ill. Nurse it a bit, Twiddle. I've got to get the tea. But mind it isn't ill all over you.'

The cat jumped up on Twiddle's knee. He looked at her with disgust – always going in and out and jumping up and down – never still for a moment. As soon as Mrs Twiddle went out of the room he pushed her off, and flapped her away with his paper.

'Sssss!' he hissed at her, 'Go away. I'll shut you into the boot cupboard again, if you're not careful – without a meat pie this time! Ssssssss!'

Chapter 8

Mr Twiddle and the Dogs

'It's a very funny thing, Twiddle,' said Mrs Twiddle, 'but I always notice that if anyone ever brings a dog here, it never goes to you. It always makes a fuss of me.'

Mr Twiddle felt cross. 'It's merely because you make a fuss of the dog,' he said. 'Anyway, my love, you always make such a dreadful fuss of our cat that it has quite turned me against making a fuss of any creature, dog, cat or horse.'

'That's not the true reason,' said Mrs Twiddle, indignantly. 'You know perfectly well that cats don't like you, and dogs don't either. I don't think that's very nice Twiddle. I think there must be something wrong with you.'

Mr Twiddle put down his newspaper. 'There's nothing wrong with me,' he said. 'I do like cats, but ours makes such a habit of tripping me up that I don't see why I should make a fuss of her. And I do like dogs, but, as I say, surely one person going crazy over any dog-visitor is enough. I've no doubt all the dogs would come to me if you didn't make such a fuss of them that they don't even know I'm here!'

'Very well,' said Mrs Twiddle. 'Very well, Twiddle. The very next time any dog comes I will hardly take any notice of it at all – but you'll see, it will still come to me and not to you.'

'You are quite wrong, my love,' said Twiddle, and began to read his newspaper again.

'Now listen, Twiddle,' said Mrs Twiddle. 'I'm certain I'm right and you're certain I'm wrong. Very well – if I prove right you must give me a new hat. And if you prove right I'll give you a new scarf.'

Mr Twiddle didn't like the sound of that at all. He had a kind of feeling that all dogs would go fawning round dear, kind, plump little Mrs Twiddle. There was something about her that animals and children couldn't resist. He sighed.

'Why do you pester me so? Very well – I'll buy you a new hat if you're right. Now, do let me read my newspaper, and stop talking about dogs.'

Mr Twiddle didn't really think much more about all this till he saw his wife looking at a hat catalogue – and to his horror he noticed that she had put a cross beside a very pretty hat. Goodness gracious, it was ten pounds! Mr Twiddle began to feel alarmed.

'Suppose she makes me buy such a very expensive hat?' he thought. 'I wouldn't be able to buy any tobacco for my pipe for about three months. This will never do. I must think hard.'

So he thought hard for a day or two, and then he suddenly stopped looking worried. He felt that he knew what to do. So he went to the butcher and bought a nice fifty pence bone that just fitted neatly into his right-hand trouser-pocket without showing. He put it there, and patted it. Aha! Dogs would feel very friendly towards him now!

That very day his wife's sister came, bringing with her a little yappy poodle. 'Oh, darling!' said Mrs Twiddle, and held out her hands to it.

It began to run to her – but half-way to Mrs Twiddle it stopped and sniffed. What was that Perfectly Delicious Smell coming from over on the right, where that man was sitting with his newspaper? Sniff-sniff! Lovely smell!

The dog dodged away from Mrs Twiddle and ran to Mr Twiddle. Ah – the smell was here! It leapt straight up on to Twiddle's knee and began to lick him.

'Well, I never!' said Mrs Twiddle, astonished. 'Look at that!'

Twiddle smiled broadly. He put the dog down. 'Go to Missus, then,' he said. 'Go to Missus and say how-de-do!'

But no – the dog only wanted to be near this exciting bone-smell.

Where was it? It leapt up again on to Mr Twiddle and made a fuss of him.

'I'm afraid that's one up to you, Twiddle,' said Mrs Twiddle, surprised and not very pleased. 'What a very peculiar thing!'

'Not at all. Probably likes my smell,' said Twiddle truthfully, and pushed the dog away again.

The next day old Mrs Dally came in,

bringing with her a rather muddy spaniel. 'Oh, the dear boy!' cooed Mrs Twiddle. 'The beautiful, long-eared boy!'

But the beautiful long-eared boy didn't give her even a glance. It gave one delightful sniff and flew to Mr Twiddle. Forty pounds of very muddy, rather smelly dog leapt on to his plump knees, and licked him vigorously from hair to chin. Mr Twiddle fended him off.

'Don't! Oooh, you're a very drippy dog. Take your tongue away from my nose. I've already washed my face once this morning. Go away, I tell you! You smell!'

'Funny that my darling doggy has taken such a fancy to your husband when he doesn't like dogs, isn't it?' said Mrs Dally, who wasn't pleased to hear her dog called smelly.

'It is peculiar,' agreed Mrs Twiddle, puzzled and rather upset. Could it be that Mr Twiddle really did attract dogs after all? Look at that spaniel now – snuffing all over him, sniff-snuff-sniffle-snuffle! Why, anyone would think it was his own dog!

The spaniel could smell the bone in Mr Twiddle's trouser-pocket and was thrilled. It scrabbled and scraped at him, licking him and flapping its long ears about till Twiddle could bear it no longer. He rose suddenly from his chair and the dog fell to the floor.

'If there's one thing worse than a man making a silly fuss of a dog, it's a dog making a silly fuss of a man!' he said. 'Now dear, perhaps you'll say I'm right and you're wrong – dogs do prefer me!'

'They certainly seem to,' said Mrs Twiddle. 'Oh, dear – now I'll have to buy you the scarf and go without that dear little hat!'

Mr Twiddle looked at her. Well, if she was going to buy him a scarf, he would buy her a hat – but not that very expensive one – oh, no!

'Listen, my love,' he said. 'You can buy me the scarf, as I am right and you are wrong; but I'll buy you a hat, though not more than five pounds will I spend! Just to show you that I'm a kind and generous husband!'

'Oh, you are, you are!' cried Mrs Twiddle, and she ran to hug him. The spaniel leapt at them both, still trying to get to Mrs Twiddle's trouser-pocket. That bone! Oh, how good it smelt!

'Well, I still can't understand my doggy making a fuss of Mr Twiddle,' said Mrs Dally, annoyed. 'He's never done that before.'

Now, the next day, Mr and Mrs Twiddle set off to buy the scarf and the hat. They bought the scarf, a nice dark-blue one with white spots. Mr Twiddle fancied himself very much in it. Then they went off to the hat shop.

Now, on the way, who should they meet but little Mr Trot with his great big Alsatian dog. Mrs Twiddle always said she didn't know if Mr Trot was taking the dog for a walk, or if the dog was taking Mr Trot for one.

Mr Twiddle suddenly remembered the bone in his trouser-pocket. He had forgotten to take it out! He began to cross the road in a hurry, before the Alsatian could smell it. But Mrs Twiddle pulled him back.

'We must just have a word with Mr Trot, dear,' she said. 'And we must pat his lovely Alsatian.'

Mr Twiddle didn't want to do anything of the sort, but it was too late to retreat now. The great dog had already caught a whiff of the rather smelly bone. It bounded at Mr Twiddle with a bark of welcome and almost knocked him over. Little Mr Trot was pulled violently along on the lead.

'Get down, you brute! Hey, get down! Stop it! Don't poke me in the face with your

81

clumsy paws!' yelled Mr Twiddle, fending the big dog away. But the Alsatian was certain that Mr Twiddle was a long-lost friend, a friend with a delicious bony smell, someone who would very soon produce the bone, if only the Alsatian could make a big enough fuss of him.

Mr Trot tugged at the lead. The dog took no notice. He leapt at Mr Twiddle again, his tongue out, and Mr Twiddle went down like a skittle. Bang! He was full-length on the pavement, squirming away from the excited dog.

Mrs Twiddle was absolutely astounded to see a dog making such a fuss of Twiddle – even knocking him over in his affection! Good gracious! But she didn't like to see Twiddle on the ground, so she poked the dog with her umbrella.

'Stop it, stop it! Let him get up!'

The Alsatian was worrying at Twiddle's right-hand trouser-pocket. He tore it. He snapped at the bone there and pulled it out, together with Twiddle's handkerchief, a tobacco pouch and a five pound note. Woof! What a bone!

After that Mr Trot found it easy to manage his enormous dog. The Alsatian was quite willing to trot home quietly, with his smelly bone, and off he went, dragging his little master behind him.

Mrs Twiddle helped Twiddle up. She looked at him very crossly indeed. 'I saw what you had in your pocket,' she said. 'A bone! You are a fraud, Twiddle. A great big shocking fraud! That's why the dogs made such a fuss of you – just because you put a bone in your pocket. I'm ashamed of you! You've got a new scarf out of me unfairly. You – you – you– oh, dear, I'm going to cry!'

But Twiddle couldn't bear that. He put his arm round plump little Mrs Twiddle and gave her a squeeze.

'What are you crying for?' he said. 'It was just a silly joke. Come on – we're going to buy that five-pound hat. Cheer up!'

So Mrs Twiddle cheered up at once, and smiled happily. 'You're a very silly man,' she said. 'Very silly indeed. But sometimes I think you're quite nice. Oh, Twiddle, don't go putting bones in your pocket again – you've no idea how they will make your clothes smell!'

'You needn't worry. I shall never do that again,' said Twiddle, trotting along. 'You can have all the fussy dogs there are. I don't want any!'

Chapter 9

Mrs Twiddle's Umbrella

'I'm just going out to fetch my paper,' Mr Twiddle called to Mrs Twiddle. 'I won't be long.'

'Take your umbrella, then, because it's raining hard,' called back Mrs Twiddle.

Twiddle looked for his umbrella. He couldn't find it anywhere. It wasn't in the hall-stand, it wasn't hanging up with his coat, it wasn't upstairs in his bedroom.

'That tiresome umbrella!' muttered Mr Twiddle to himself. 'It's always disappearing Could I have left it anywhere, I wonder?'

He thought hard. He might have left it at the post office. He might have left it at the butcher's. He might have left it at the fishmonger's. There were any amount of places where he had already left it at one time or another, and might have left it again the last time it rained.

Twiddle felt guilty. Mrs Twiddle always had a lot to say when he couldn't find his umbrella. She would make him go and ask at every shop in the town if she knew it wasn't in the hall-stand.

'Haven't you gone yet?' called Mrs Twiddle. 'Do go, dear. I want you back in good time for dinner, you know. And bring back some fish for the cat, will you?'

'All right,' called Twiddle. 'Though I don't know why that cat should have so much fish. It has far more than we do. And I do hate carrying fish home on a wet day. It smells so, and – '

'Now, Twiddle, take a basket and go,' called Mrs Twiddle. 'Do you want me to come and button your coat and find your hat and put up your umbrella for you? Really, if I don't you'll never get away this morning.'

Twiddle looked once more at the hall-stand in despair. Where, oh, where was his tiresome umbrella? He heard Mrs Twiddle coming, and he snatched at the only umbrella in the stand. It belonged to Mrs Twiddle. Never mind, he would borrow it just this once.

He rushed out of the front door and banged it behind him. He buttoned his coat and put up his umbrella as he went down the path, afraid that Mrs Twiddle might call him back. She would be very cross if she knew he couldn't find his own umbrella and had taken hers.

Mr Twiddle went to get his paper. He stuffed it into his pocket because he didn't want it to get wet. Then he actually remembered to call at the fish-shop for some fish for the cat. Twiddle didn't like his wife's cat. It always sat just where he could fall over it.

The fishmonger stuffed some fish-heads and fishtails into a bit of paper. Mr Twiddle took the parcel in disgust. Why hadn't he brought a basket as Mrs Twiddle had suggested? Now, his hands would smell of fish all day.

He put up his umbrella again and walked off down the street. Somebody called to him: 'Hey, Mr Twiddle! The sun is out and the rain's stopped. Why have you got your umbrella up?'

Twiddle stopped at once, feeling very

foolish. Yes, it is a lovely sunny morning now, and he hadn't noticed. He tried to put the umbrella down with one hand, because he had the fish in the other, but he couldn't. It was too stiff. So he put the fish on a wall for a moment and then managed to put the umbrella down.

'Meeow!' said a delighted voice, and a big tabby cat jumped up beside the fish. It tore at the bit of paper that wrapped it.

'Stop that!' said Twiddle, crossly, and gave the cat a prod with his umbrella. It yowled, and disappeared, taking with it the bit of paper the fish had been wrapped in.

'Bother!' said Twiddle annoyed. 'Now the

fish hasn't got any paper – look at all the heads and tails slithering about on the wall. I can't carry them like that.'

He remembered his own newspaper safely stuffed in his pocket. He'd have to wrap the fish in that. How horrid! Still, there was nothing else to be done.

Twiddle carefully hooked his wife's umbrella in the branch of a tree that hung down over the wall. He wrapped the fish-scraps in his paper, and walked off down the street.

He left his wife's umbrella behind him, of course. He never once thought of it until the rain suddenly began to fall again. Then he found he hadn't an umbrella to put up!

'Oh, my! I hooked it on to that branch by the wall where I wrapped up the fish in my paper,' he groaned, and rushed back to get it.

But it wasn't there. Not a sign of an umbrella could he see! He called out to the woman in the little sweet-shop opposite.

'Did you see anyone take an umbrella from this branch here? I left it not long ago.'

'Oh, yes,' called back the sweet-shop woman. 'Somebody took it not five minutes ago.'

'The thief!' said Twiddle, indignantly. 'What was he like?'

'It wasn't a he, it was a she,' said the woman. 'It was somebody dressed in a blue mackintosh and a hat with daisies on. She was rather plump, and hurried along like anything.'

'Thank you!' called Twiddle. 'I'll track down that nasty woman if it takes me all morning!'

So off he went, hunting for a plump woman in a blue mackintosh and a hat with daisies on it. He couldn't see her anywhere. He stopped a man on a corner and asked him if he had seen anyone dressed like that.

'Yes,' said the man. 'She passed me at the bottom of that road. She was going towards the bicycle shop, if you know where that is.'

Twiddle did. He raced along to the bicycle shop, getting wetter and wetter as the rain poured down. He felt very angry indeed. To think that that thief of a woman should steal his wife's umbrella and send him on a goose-chase like this in the pouring rain.

He went into the shop. 'Did somebody wearing a blue mackintosh and a hat with daisies on come in here?' he asked.

'Somebody with a very nice umbrella – with a dog's head on the crook-handle?'

'Yes,' said the boy there. 'She did. She said she was going down to the baker's – you might get her there.'

Off went Twiddle to the baker's. He peered inside. Nobody there at all. 'What do you want?' called the baker's wife.

'Somebody in a blue mackintosh and a hat with daisies,' called Twiddle in despair.

'Oh, she came in for a cake just now,' said the woman. 'She's only just gone. Hurry round the corner and you'll catch her!'

Twiddle hurried – ah, there was somebody in a blue mackintosh and hat with daisies, scurrying along with an umbrella up – his wife's umbrella, too! How dared the woman be such a thief? She deserved to go to prison.

At that very moment Mr Plod, the policeman, came round a corner and nearly bumped into Twiddle.

'Morning, Mr Twiddle,' said Mr Plod. 'How wet you are! I thought only policemen had to go out in the rain without umbrellas!'

'Mr Plod, you're just the man I want,' said Mr Twiddle, eagerly. 'Someone's stolen my wife's umbrella, and the thief is there – look,

91

down the road in front of us – with the very umbrella! What shall I do?'

'I'll deal with this,' said Mr Plod. 'That's what policemen are for. Come along with me, sir.'

So Mr Plod and Mr Twiddle hurried after the thief in the blue mackintosh. Aha! She would soon be very frightened indeed.

'There – she's gone into Mrs Chatter's house,' said Mr Plod. 'We'll have to go and knock at the door and get in and face her. Come along.'

Mr Plod knocked loudly at the door. Mrs Chatter opened it and Mr Plod walked in.

Mr Twiddle stayed at the front door. He thought he would let Mr Plod deal with this. He heard the policeman's rumbling voice.

'I've had a report that an umbrella has been stolen,' he said. 'Was it you, madam, who took it?'

A voice answered him indignantly. 'Yes, it was me – and why shouldn't I take it? It was my own umbrella! There it was, hanging on the branch of a tree in the middle of the village street – my umbrella! I'd like to know who put it there! Just wait till I find out who took my umbrella and hung it on a tree in the village street!'

'Dear me,' said Mr Plod. 'Are you sure it was your own umbrella? What is your name, madam?'

'You know my name quite well – I'm Mrs Twiddle!' said the voice indignantly.

Well, Mr Twiddle could have told Mr Plod that, of course. He knew his wife's voice very well indeed. He stood shivering at the front door, feeling very upset indeed.

'You wait till Mr Twiddle hears about this,' went on Mrs Twiddle. 'He went out this morning with his own umbrella – a little later I remembered I had to go out too. But I couldn't find my umbrella at all, so I put on my oldest hat and my mackintosh and out I went without one. And just *imagine* how astonished I was suddenly to see my very own umbrella hanging on a tree in the village street! I couldn't believe my eyes.'

'Very strange,' agreed the policeman, wondering what Mr Twiddle was going to say about all this.

'And now you come banging at my friend's door and tell me somebody says I've stolen my own umbrella!' went on Mrs Twiddle. 'I never heard anything like it. Show me the person who says I stole it, and I'll show you the thief – it must be he who took my umbrella and hung it on that tree! He must be mad. He must be –'

Twiddle didn't wait to hear any more. Feeling very sick indeed, he stole off down the path. He hoped Mr Plod wouldn't give him away. If only he could get home before Mrs Twiddle discovered anything more!

Mr Plod didn't give him away. He apologised to Mrs Twiddle and went off in a hurry before she could ask him any awkward questions. Mrs Twiddle went home with her umbrella, very cross indeed.

Twiddle had got there first. He had opened the front door and had fallen over the cat, who, as usual, loved to sit in the very middle of the dark hall.

The cat sniffed at him. He smelt very pleasantly of fish. Twiddle felt about for the fish he had bought.

But he hadn't got it. He had left it on the wall when he had gone back to look for the umbrella!

'If you think I'm going back there to look for your fish, you're mistaken, Cat,' he said. But then he remembered that his morning paper was round the fish – and he wouldn't be able to read the news if he didn't get the fish!

He groaned and went to the front door again, followed by the excited cat.

He peered out. It was pouring with rain. He stepped out valiantly into it – and bumped into Mrs Twiddle hurrying down the path with her umbrella up!

'Twiddle, you're not going out again, are you?' she cried. 'I've got such a lot to tell you. Why are you going out again?'

'I've forgotten the cat's fish,' said Twiddle, desperately.

'Oh, never mind for once,' said Mrs Twiddle, anxious to tell Twiddle the story of her umbrella and Mr Plod.

'I must go and get it,' said Twiddle and shook himself away from his wife.

'Oh, Twiddle, it's very kind of you, but the cat can go without for once!' cried Mrs Twiddle. 'Come back. Where's your umbrella?'

'I don't know,' said Twiddle, in despair.

'But, Twiddle, you went out with your umbrella this morning – I saw you!' cried Mrs Twiddle. 'Oh, Twiddle, have you lost it again? Did you come home without it? Here take mine.'

'No, no, NO!' shouted Twiddle, who felt that he could never touch his wife's umbrella again. 'I'd rather get soaked!'

And off went poor old Twiddle into the rain to get back the fish and his paper. But the tabby cat had been there before him, so he won't find either. Really, he is a most unlucky fellow, isn't he?

Mr Twiddle In Trouble Again

Mr Twiddle is a kind old man who means to do his best, but he is often forgetful, a bit lazy and sometimes very silly. Poor Mrs Twiddle is driven to distraction by his muddles.

This time he accidentally sells his boots, puts fish in his wardrobe and mistakes a burglar for his pet cat.

Age 6+

£2.99

award publications limited

ISBN 1-84135-299-3

9 781841 352992